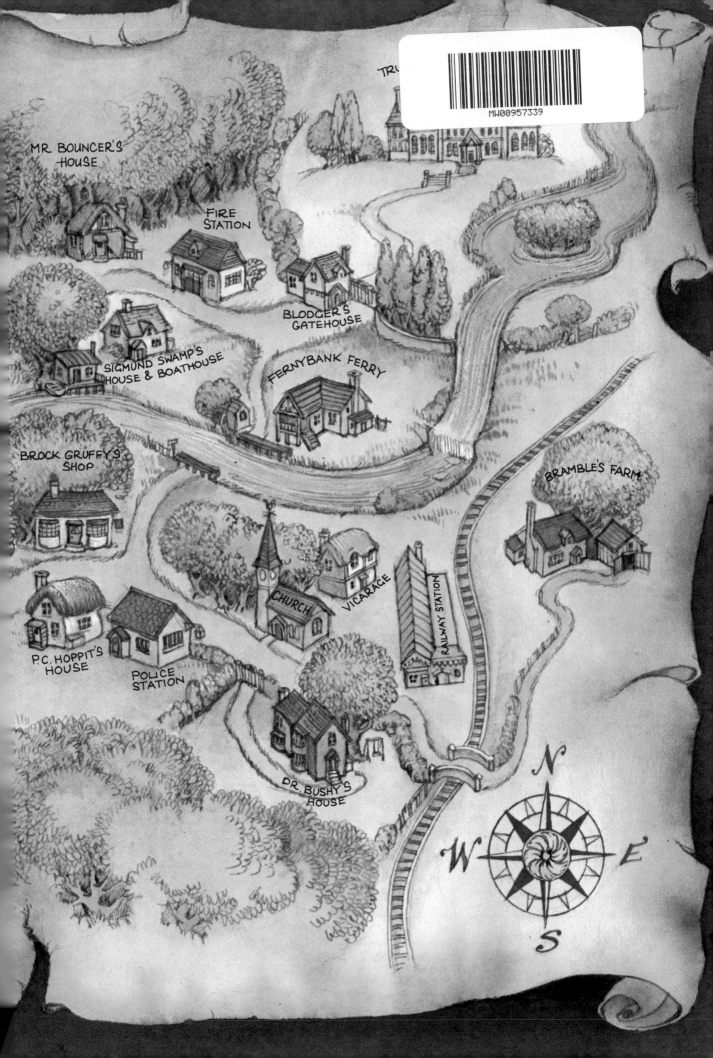

CONTENTS

PUBLISHED BY PETER HADDOCK LIMITED, BRIDLINGTON, ENGLAND.
© FERN HOLLOW PRODUCTIONS LIMITED
PRINTED IN INDIA

SPIKE AND THE
COWBOY BAND

Spike Willowbank was on his way to see Sigmund Swamp for his music lesson. Spike played the violin and was looking forward to performing in the Fern Hollow Music Festival later that week. The hedgehog turned a corner in the lane and was surprised by a couple of his friends who were racing down the hill in their billycarts and almost knocked him over. "Hello, Spike!" said Patch. "Come and play on the carts with us." "Sorry, I can't," said Spike. "I have to go to my music lesson." "Yuck!" said Patch. "Music is boring." "Yes," agreed Monty. "Billycarts are much more fun!" Spike wondered if his friends might be right, but he continued on his way to Sigmund's house.

"Good morning, Spike," said Sigmund. "Are you looking forward to the Music Festival?" "Oh yes, of course!" replied Spike, though by now he was not so sure. "Jolly good," said the toad. "Let me hear the piece you've been practising." Spike began to play but, after a time, his concentration was broken by a loud snoring noise. He glanced across at Sigmund and discovered that he had fallen fast asleep. "Oh dear," sighed Spike. "This must be a very boring piece of music if it sends the teacher to sleep!"

At Trundleberry Manor the Fern Hollow Brass Band was practising their contribution to the Music Festival. "Yes, that was very good," said Lord Trundle when the band had stopped playing. "I think the festival will be a great success. As well as the band there will be all the other contributions: Mr Periwinkle will play his flute; there will be the recorder group and Spike Willowbank will play his violin." "I agree," said Brock Gruffy. "It will be very entertaining, but it would be nice if we could think of something to make it a little different this year." "Mmmm, you're right," said Lord Trundle. "Listen, I think I have an idea."

The next day Spike and his friends were fishing in the River Ferny when Jingle's taxi drew up close by at the Jolly Vole Hotel. They all watched as Jingle opened the door for his passengers and they stepped out. They were four animals dressed like cowboys. One of them, a raccoon, tipped Jingle and then they all disappeared into the hotel. "Wow!" cried Patch. "They look great. I wonder if they're real cowboys."

That night as Spike lay in bed he heard music drifting across from the Jolly Vole. It was the sort of music that cowboys play. "Of course," said Spike, "they are a Cowboy Band. That's wonderful!" Spike was very excited. He crept out of the house and ran down the lane to the hotel. The music was coming from one of the upstairs rooms. Spike clambered up a tree and peeped in through the window.

The band was practising. They sounded marvellous! The music was very jolly, the sort of thing that would make you want to dance. In fact, Spike began to rock and jiggle around in the tree. That was a mistake because suddenly the hedgehog lost his balance and fell. Fortunately, his pyjamas caught on a branch and he was left dangling high above the ground. "Help!" cried Spike. "Somebody get me down!" The landlord of the Jolly Vole and the Cowboy Band quickly came rushing out to see what all the noise was about. "Don't worry, pardner!" shouted Rip, the bandleader. "I'll get you down!" Rip at once began to shin up the tree.

He climbed out on to the branch on which Spike was caught and pulled him up. Everyone cheered, but the next moment there was a loud crack, the branch broke and they both fell down to the ground! Spike was all right – he landed on top of Rip, who broke his fall – but the raccoon himself was not so lucky. He had badly hurt one arm. Doctor Bushy came and put it in a sling. "I'm afraid you won't be able to play the fiddle for a while," he said. "Darn it," said Rip. "Lord Trundle invited us here to play in your Music Festival. What are we going to do now?" "I can play the violin," said Spike. "Perhaps you could teach me some of your music and I could be in the Cowboy Band." "Well, I guess we could try it," agreed Rip.

The next day was Music Festival day. Mr Chips, the carpenter, had built a little bandstand in one of Farmer Bramble's fields. The Fern Hollow Brass Band played their music there all afternoon.

Later, in the evening, came the special event – the Barn Dance. "And now," cried Lord Trundle, "I give you Spike and the Cowboy Band!" Spike had managed to learn the music. Though Rip couldn't play his fiddle he could still call for the dances and the Fern Hollow animals had a real hoe-down! You can just imagine how impressed Spike's friends were! They certainly never said anything about music being boring, ever again!

THE MYSTERIOUS FORTUNE TELLERS

The day before the village fête was all hustle and bustle. The Fern Hollow animals were busy preparing their entries for the various competitions. Mrs Tuttleebee and her daughter, Heather, were baking a blackberry pie.

Brock Gruffy was
tending his marrow

and Spike Willowbank was putting the finishing
touches to his painting.

The morning of the fête was bright and clear and everyone was bubbling over with excitement. There were stalls selling all kinds of things. The refreshment tent had been put up and Farmer Bramble was taking children for rides on Hazel, the donkey. But the thing that aroused the most interest was the funny, little tent in the far corner of the field and the peculiar person standing at its entrance. He had a big, black beard and wore a turban and baggy trousers. "Come and have your fortune told by the Gypsy!" he cried. "The world-famous fortune-teller will gaze into her crystal ball and foretell your future." "I'll give it a try," said Brock Gruffy.

Brock was ushered into the dimly-lit tent where the mysterious gypsy sat hunched over her crystal ball. She wore a big hood and it was difficult to see her face. "Ah, I see you are a shop keeper," she said. Her voice was surprisingly deep. "How on earth did you know that?" gasped Brock. The gypsy began to chant:

"Your Past and Future I can see,
Everything that's yet to be.
The fortune-teller sees it all
Swirling in the crystal ball.
Cross my palm with silver, please."

Brock handed her a silver coin and was delighted to be told that he was certain to win the vegetable competition.

The fortune-teller was very popular. All the animals went to see her. She began each time by telling them something about themselves that some-one from a land far away could not possibly have known without a crystal ball. Then she went on to tell them their futures. The gypsy's money jar was soon full to the brim.

"I think we'd best be off now before we're rumbled," growled the fortune-teller. She threw back her hood and revealed herself to be that rascally weasel, Snitch. "You're right," chuckled her assistant who was, of course, Snatch. "This false beard is beginning to tickle anyway!"

Outside, in the sunshine, Lord Trundle was judging the vegetable competition. "After due consideration," he said, "the first prize for the best vegetable goes to Mr Prickles's cauliflower." "That can't be right. The fortune-teller said my marrow would win!" cried Brock Gruffy. "She told me my turnip would win," complained Grandpa Bouncer. "She's a fraud!" exclaimed Mr Periwinkle. "She told all of us we would win!"

When it came to the painting competition, Spike was very upset to find that his painting only came second. "But the fortune-teller said that I would win," he sobbed.

Things were getting rather uncomfortable for Lord Trundle. He hurried off to the baking competition. "The first prize for the best cake goes to Mrs Bouncer's carrot cake," declared Lord Trundle. "That's outrageous!" exclaimed Mrs Tuttleebee. "The fortune-teller said I would win!" "Oh dear," sighed Lord Trundle. Meanwhile, Hazel, the donkey, was feeling a little peckish and, taking advantage of the confusion, she decided to help herself to Mrs Willowbank's jam sponge. Unfortunately she did not notice that the jam had attracted a number of wasps.

As she bit into the cake the angry wasps stung
Hazel's nose! The poor donkey brayed loudly and
rushed off through the fête with the wasps still
buzzing around her head and Farmer Bramble
chasing after her.

CRASH! Hazel plunged headlong into the fortune-tellers' tent. Snitch and Snatch were astonished. They were kicked by Hazel and stung by the wasps! Now everyone could see that it was Snitch and Snatch who had tricked them. "Well, they're getting exactly what they deserve," laughed Sigmund Swamp.

The two wicked weasels ran away, leaving the money behind them, and were not seen in Fern Hollow for a long time afterwards, and poor, old Hazel had some nice, cool lotion put on her nose. The money was given to Parson Dimly for repairs to the church roof which, as usual, needed doing.

It had been a fête to remember!

CASTAWAYS ON HERON ISLAND

It was the morning of the school nature trip. Miss Crisp was taking her class for a visit to Heron Island, which is the little island in the middle of the River Ferny on the Trundleberry Manor Estate.

At Buttercup Cottage the Bouncer Family was in a terrible panic. Patch couldn't find his shoes. They had all hunted high and low without success. "You'll make us late for school," wailed Pippa. "We'll miss the trip." "Don't worry," sighed Mrs Bouncer. "Here they are in the washing basket." "How did they get there?" said Patch. "Oh, I expect they walked!" chuckled Mrs Bouncer. "Come along now, here are your school books. Away you go." She stood at the cottage door and waved them goodbye and off they skipped.

Miss Crisp led her class, walking in pairs, down the dusty, little road to Trundleberry Manor. When they arrived they found Lord Trundle up a ladder inspecting his roof. He came down shaking his head sadly. "The roof is in a terrible state," he said. "In fact, the whole of Trundleberry Manor is in desperate need of repair. Unfortunately I have no money to pay for it! But I don't suppose you want to listen to my troubles. You've come for your nature trip to Heron Island, haven't you?"

Miss Crisp and her class followed Lord Trundle down to the River Ferny where they found a little boat waiting for them. Everyone climbed on board and Lord Trundle cast off and started the engine. "First stop, Heron Island," he cried. The children cheered loudly. They were all very excited. Patch and Pippa peered over the side of the boat down into the dark, green water, where they could see the fish darting around beneath them. Patch thought he caught a glimpse of a big, green pike sliding by. "It was just like a submarine," he said.

From the island, hidden amongst the tall reeds, a strange bird watched the boat approaching. It was Old Man Heron. He was a solitary sort of gentleman

and not at all pleased to have his peace and quiet
spoiled by a lot of noisy school-children. He would
have to keep an eye on them. He watched as the
boat pulled up to the shore and the children and
Miss Crisp climbed out. "Have a nice time," said
Lord Trundle. "I'll be back to collect you later this
afternoon."

"Gather round, children," said Miss Crisp. "Pay close attention now. When we are walking around the island, I would like you to make lists of all the sorts of flowers, birds and butterflies you see. When we get back to school tomorrow we will do some writing about them and make a wall frieze. Stay together now. Off we go!"

The children set off down the woodland path with Miss Crisp leading the way and pointing out things of interest. They were deep in the forest when Patch suddenly tripped over his shoe lace. Pippa giggled. "You did that!" cried Patch. "You tripped me up." "Of course I didn't," replied Pippa. "You did," growled Patch and the next moment they were fighting. Meanwhile Miss Crisp and the rest of the class didn't notice the quarrelling rabbits and continued on their way.

43

When Pippa and Patch finally broke off from their fighting they realised they had been left behind and ran to catch up. But the pathway split in two directions and they took the wrong one. Soon they were hopelessly lost.

The island suddenly began to seem strange and spooky. The trees appeared more twisty, their branches reaching out as if to grab the frightened little rabbits, and from time to time Pippa and Patch caught sight of Old Man Heron watching them with his black, beady eyes. It was late now and growing rather cold. The two exhausted rabbits took shelter amongst the roots of an old tree.

As they huddled together to keep warm, Patch and Pippa heard a rustling in the undergrowth and out stepped Old Man Heron, looking very severe. "I have been watching you," he said. "You have been very silly. Your teacher and the rest of your class left the island long ago without noticing you were missing." "Then how will we get home?" wailed Pippa. "We are marooned! Castaways!" "Don't worry," said Old Man Heron. "I know a way. Follow me."

Pippa and Patch followed the strange bird to a hollow tree with steps inside it leading down into the earth. "Take this lantern and follow the tunnel," said Old Man Heron. "It will lead you to safety." The rabbits thanked the heron, said goodbye and crept down the steps. The tunnel was narrow and low and seemed to go on for ever but at last it came to an end and there, above their heads, they found a small doorway. Patch pushed it open.

The rabbits climbed through the doorway and found themselves standing in a strange room filled with all kinds of peculiar and interesting objects. There was a rocking horse, a suit of armour, an old painting of a fox cavalier and lots and lots of other things. Pippa found a chest filled with funny old clothes which they both had a marvellous time trying on!

After a time they began to look around for a way out of the room. There was no obvious doorway. "What's this?" said Pippa, pulling a lever in the wall.

Suddenly a panel swung open, revealing a startled Lord Trundle, sitting in his living room. "We're in Trundleberry Manor!" gasped Patch. Lord Trundle was amazed. He had not known about the secret room. "Good gracious!" he exclaimed, noticing the painting of the cavalier. "Do you know, I believe that is 'The Laughing Fox Cavalier'. It was painted by one of my ancestors and has been lost for a hundred years. It is worth a fortune!"

Lord Trundle was perfectly right. He sold the painting to Poppletown Museum and the money more than paid for the repairs to Trundleberry Manor. His troubles were over. As for Patch and Pippa, they had their photographs taken with 'The Laughing Fox Cavalier' by Poppletown newspaper. The headline above the photograph read, "Castaways on Heron Island find Famous Picture".

THE FLOATING RESTAURANT

One morning Brock Gruffy received a letter from his cousin, Bill. It read:

Dear Brock,
    As you know, I am very fond of sailing. Recently I have acquired a new boat and I thought you might like my old one. You'll find it on the river, by the old jetty.
    Happy sailing!
Yours, Bill.

When Brock saw the boat he was rather disappointed. It was badly in need of repair. But the badger was struck with a wonderful idea. "I'll turn it into a floating restaurant," he thought.

So, with the help of his old friend Sigmund Swamp, who was very keen to be the waiter on the floating restaurant, Brock set to work.

"It's perfect," said Sigmund when the repairs were finished. "All we need now are customers!"

Sigmund drew up some posters to advertise the restaurant and Brock went round the village pasting them up. That evening the first customers arrived. They were the Bouncers and the Willowbanks, having a meal out to celebrate Mr Willowbank's birthday. Sigmund took the orders and, while Brock was busy with the cooking, he played his piano accordion and sang. It was not a great success, but Sigmund didn't appear to notice this.

Brock soon had the cooking done. Sigmund served the meal and everyone was delighted. "Delicious!" exclaimed Mrs Bouncer. "I do love carrot stew, don't you?"

Later, Sigmund appeared with a beautiful birthday cake which Brock had cooked in advance for Mr Willowbank. By this time a wind had sprung up and the water was getting a bit choppy. The barge was rolling a little and, as he came across the deck, Sigmund lost his balance. His feet shot from under him and the cake flew up into the air and came down on top of Mr Willowbank's head!

"Whoops!" said Sigmund. "Happy Birthday."

The customers left the restaurant in a very bad
mood indeed. "Well, that's that," said Brock.
"No-one's going to want to eat here again." It
was getting late so Brock and Sigmund decided to
call it a day. They climbed into their bunks and
fell fast asleep.

In the night the wind grew steadily stronger. It
began to rain. The thunder rolled and the
lightning flashed. Then CRASH, an old tree was
struck and fell into the river. The fallen tree
dammed up the river and the water began to rise.
At last the River Ferny burst its banks and
poured down into Fern Hollow, carrying the
restaurant and the sleeping friends with it!

Sigmund and Brock awoke next morning to the
sound of frenzied hooting and cries for help.
Imagine their surprise when they went up on
deck and found themselves floating through Fern
Hollow, just outside Boris Blinks's book shop!
The village was flooded.

Boris and Leapy Lizard had taken refuge up on
their rooftop. Precarious piles of valuable books
which they had managed to save were balanced
all around them. "Hoot, hoot! Save us, save us!"
cried Boris, flapping his wings hysterically.

Sigmund and Brock lost no time in beginning
the rescue operation. After Boris and Leapy
there were many other animals to help. Everyone
in the village had been forced to take refuge up
in their bedrooms or on their rooftops. Sigmund
and Brock took them on board and ferried them
to the safety of higher ground.

Later, the two heroes discovered the fallen tree damming up the river. "That's the cause of the flood," said Sigmund. "I think we are going to need the help of Farmer Bramble to move it."

Bramble Farm was on high ground and had not been affected by the flood. The farmer soon arrived on his tractor. He attached a strong chain to the tree and pulled it out of the river.

Now the Ferny was flowing freely again. The floodwater would go down, but that would take some time. Meanwhile the Fern Hollow animals were all sitting around, feeling miserable.

"I know how to cheer everyone up," said Brock, and he disappeared down into the galley. A little while later the air was filled with the delicious smell of his cooking. Brock had made a marvellous vegetable casserole – enough to feed the whole village. Suddenly everyone was happy again. There would be lots of work to do, cleaning up Fern Hollow when the floodwater had gone down, but in the meantime they were all having fun at the floating restaurant.

64

The Midsummer Banquet

In a few days it would be time for the Midsummer Banquet to be held at Trundleberry Manor. In his attic, Lord Trundle was rummaging around looking for the candelabras and punch bowl which he had stored away after the previous year's celebrations.

"Now, where did I put them," he muttered, "perhaps they are in this chest."

Opening the chest, he found, amongst many other things, an old engraving of a medieval castle — FERN HOLLOW CASTLE!

"That's rather odd," muttered Lord Trundle. "There's no castle in Fern Hollow these days. It must have fallen into ruins many years ago. But this gives me an idea. This year we will have a medieval Midsummer Banquet and everyone can come in medieval costume."

Lord Trundle lost no time in sending out the invitations and
soon everyone in the village was talking about the banquet.
Mr. and Mrs. Thimble, the Fern Hollow Tailors, were kept
extremely busy making the medieval costumes and the lights
in their windows burned late into the night. When at last the
clothes were finished the animals came to try them on. You
would hardly have recognised Brock Gruffy, Mr. Bouncer or
Mrs. Willowbank in their costumes. They looked splendid!

The morning before the banquet Lord Trundle decided that he would visit Mr. Crackleberry who would be doing the catering. He was driving along in his car when a thick mist came down. Unable to see where he was going, and still thinking that he was on the road, he drove down a narrow track into Windy Wood. After some time the track petered out and Lord Trundle's car got stuck in the mud. Then the poor fox had to get out and struggle along on foot. Suddenly the mist began to clear and, to his surprise, Lord Trundle found himself standing in front of Fern Hollow Castle.

It was the same castle as the one in Lord Trundle's
engraving. Although it was mostly in ruins, one of the towers
was still standing and naturally the fox felt that he must
explore it. As he climbed the stone staircase inside the tower,
Lord Trundle's footsteps echoed noisily, disturbing some bats
which fluttered around his head. They gave him quite a
fright. At the top of the stairs was a heavy wooden door. He
opened it and entered a dusty little room filled with suits of
armour and other interesting things. Suddenly a gust of wind
blew in through the window and slammed the door shut.
Lord Trundle tried to open it but it was locked. He was
trapped!

71

As soon as it was realised that Lord Trundle was missing, P.C. Hoppit organised a search party to find him. The clever policeman quickly deduced what had happened and the search party followed the tracks of Lord Trundle's car into Windy Wood. When at last they arrived at the Castle, they found the fox waving from the Castle window and shouting for help.

The search party had come well-equipped and a length of strong rope was quickly thrown up to Lord Trundle.
"Tie one end of it to the door handle," instructed P.C. Hoppit, "then climb down."
Lord Trundle was not accustomed to climbing down ropes but, with the encouragement of his friends, he managed to lower himself safely down to the ground. When he had recovered from his ordeal he announced that he had had a brilliant idea.
"Let's hold the Midsummer Banquet here at the Castle," he said.
"It's the perfect place for it."

75

A great deal of work was put into the preparations for the
banquet. Lots of fairy lights were hung in the trees around
the Castle and Mr. Chips made an enormous wooden table,
big enough for all the animals to sit around. On the night of
the banquet everyone turned up in their medieval costumes,
carrying lanterns. There was even medieval music supplied
by Sigmund Swamp, who played a lute and sang a few little
songs which he had written.

Finally, an enormous bonfire was lit and there was a wonderful firework display, with rockets flying up into the night sky to burst into flowers of coloured sparks above the ruins of the Castle. It was a really wonderful evening, one which the Fern Hollow animals would remember for a long, long time.

SPORTS DAY

It was still very early in the morning, but some of the Fern Hollow animals were already busily preparing for the Sports Day, which, as usual, was to be held in one of Farmer Bramble's fields. Spike and Patch had been given the job of painting the white lines for the running lanes.

Meanwhile,
on the edge of the
field, Mr. Chips whistled happily
to himself as he went about the business of
putting up a refreshments stand.
"It's beginning to look quite splendid, Mr. Chips,"
exclaimed Mr. Acorn, who was supplying the cakes and buns.
"It certainly is," agreed Mr. Crackleberry, rolling a big
barrel of orange juice off the back of his wagon.
"I hope the weather stays fine though—there's a big
black cloud over there on the horizon."

At Trundleberry Manor, Lord Trundle packed the sports day prizes into a trunk and carried them out to his car. He too noticed the dark cloud on the horizon, but he was in too much of a hurry to give it much thought and, jumping into the car, he drove off to the sports field.

Suddenly, as he was driving over the bridge by the Jolly Vole Hotel, Lord Trundle's car hit a big stone lying in the road.

It was such a hard bump
that the trunk containing
the prizes shot off the roof
rack and with a great
SPLOSH!
landed in the River Ferny.

Luckily the trunk floated, but it was soon caught in the
current and swept away down the river.
"Oh no!" panted Lord Trundle,
rushing along the river bank.
"What ever shall we do?"

84

The Sports Day prizes would
certainly have been lost if it had not
been for Sigmund Swamp, who was
out fishing, and seeing the trunk
floating by, cast out his line and
caught it, just as if it had been a
great big fish!

It turned out that Sigmund had quite forgotten that it was the Sports Day, and was very pleased when Lord Trundle offered him a lift in his car. By the time they arrived at the sports field, the tug of war was about to begin, but the big black cloud was now directly overhead.

Each of the two teams led by P.C. Hoppit and Brock Gruffy got a firm grip on the rope. Boris Blink slowly raised the starting pistol and — BANG — the contest began.

A few moments later the big black cloud burst.
The rain came pouring down and, in next to no
time, the field became waterlogged.
The tug of war teams slipped and slid around
in the mud, fell into the puddles and looked
quite ridiculous.

Everyone ran for the shelter of the trees or the refreshments stand, where they all stood around looking very glum. It looked as if the Sports Day would have to be cancelled. The sky was now completely covered with clouds and the rain was falling harder all the time!

Then Lord Trundle had a wonderful idea.
"Everyone is invited to Trundleberry Manor," he cried.
"We'll hold the Sports Day indoors!"
All the animals agreed that it was a fine idea and they
quickly made their way to the Manor.

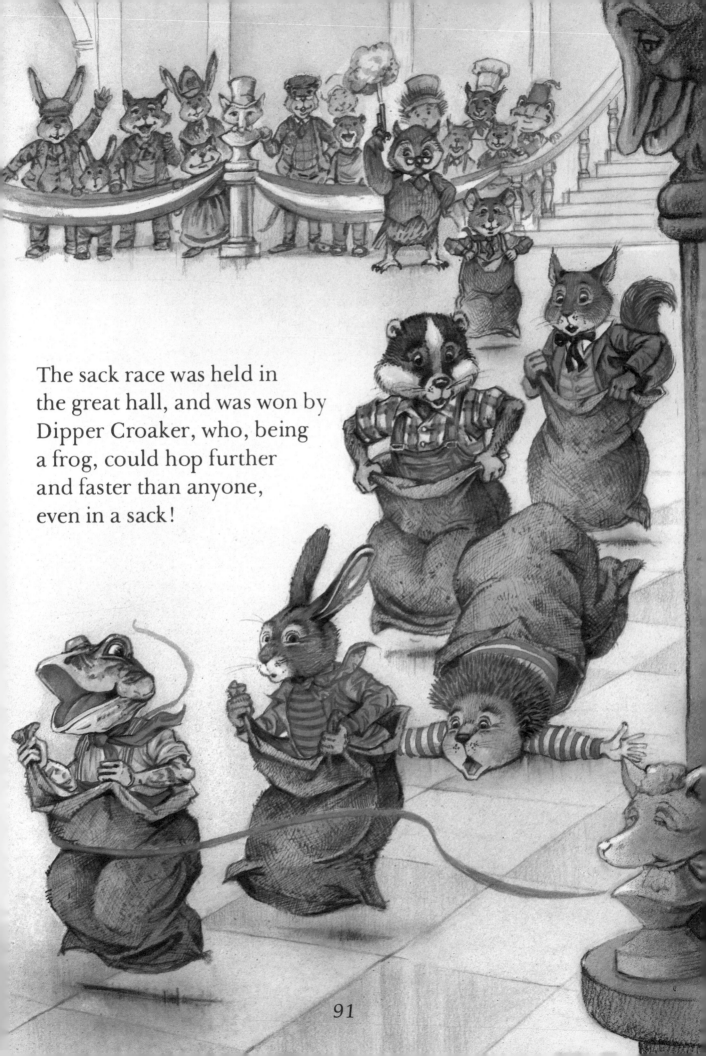

The sack race was held in
the great hall, and was won by
Dipper Croaker, who, being
a frog, could hop further
and faster than anyone,
even in a sack!

The egg and spoon race up and down the
main staircase was great fun. Clarence
Hoppit was in the lead for most of the
way, but he dropped his egg and
Dusty Rusty won by a whisker.

Then came the special event, the bannister slide. The
contestants slid down the bannister, flew off the end, and
landed on a mattress. Spike Willowbank won this quite
easily, but he overshot the mattress and landed on top of
Brock Gruffy!

When the games were all over, Sigmund Swamp set up his camera to take a picture of the prize giving ceremony. "Smile everyone," said Sigmund.

Everyone did smile and it made a marvellous picture!

Fern Hollow

MR. CHIPS'S HOUSE

MR. WILLOWBANK'S
COBBLERS SHOP

MR. CROAKER'S WATERMILL

STRIPEY'S HOUSE

SCHOOL

THE JOLLY VOLE
HOTEL

RIVER FERNY

MR. ACORN'S
BAKERY

MR. RUSTY'S HOUSE

MR. PRICKLES'S HOUSE

POST OFFICE

BORIS BLINKS'S
BOOKSHOP

MR. TWINKLE'S
HOUSE

MR. TUTTLEBEE'S
SHOP

MR. THIMBLE'S
TAILORS SHOP

WINDYWOOD